Bob and the Cyber-Llama

by Joseph Caldara

i

Bob and the Cyber-Llama

ISBN 10: 0-9984298-0-5
ISBN 13: 978-0-9984298-0-9

Edited by Joseph Caldara, Nathan Selinsky, and Jon Adams
Cover and page design by Joseph Caldara
www.bobandthecyberllama.com

Printed in the United States of America

TABLE OF CONTENTS

Chapter 1

Bob's mother had told him hundreds of times that it wasn't polite to stare, but he couldn't help it. The jowls of wrinkly fat that had overtaken his grandmother's chin undulated so much when she talked that he couldn't look away. It was like a vast, mountainous, jagged wasteland of semisolid pudding with little hairs sticking out at random intervals. He had long since forgotten what they had been talking about and was instead counting the various boils and moles like he was looking at a blubbery puzzle.

"Well, what do you have to say, Bob dear?" Grandma Edwina said, snapping Bob out of his trance.

"Uh…what was the question again, grandma?"

"I said, have you found another job yet?"

"Oh," Bob said, shifting uncomfortably on the orange leather couch, "No, grandma. I'm still working at Porkburger."

"Hm," Grandma Edwina grunted, "I don't see why. I've heard you complain about it at least eighty times.

"I know, grandma, but-"

"But nothing, Bob. You're talented. If Louis Armstrong and Carrot Top had a baby, it'd be you. What is it you'd like to do with your life?"

"I...er...don't know right now."

"That's Grade-A, USDA-approved, prime-cut bull plop, Bobby. You're my grandson! You've had a fire in your toilet-cleaner-water blue eyes ever since you were the size of dachshund. And besides, you're willing to spend more than five minutes talking to me. That has to count for something. Now what do you want to pursue more than anything in the world?"

"I'm not sure...something adventurous." Without knowing it, Bob cracked a smile, "Something exciting...and a little dangerous."

"Really...?"

2

Bob's smile vanished. "But I mean, I do need a steady job and Porkburger pays well."

"Oh. Do you need some money?"

"No, grandma," Bob said. He did need money, but he didn't like asking Grandma Edwina. And he knew she had already given quite a bit of cash to the Orphans Who Look Like Rob Schneider Fund, which meant her money management skills had likely gone the way of her good looks.

"Well, let me know if you do," she said, scratching herself, "Just don't move back in with your parents or whatever it is you young folks do these days. And remember that you have a lot going for you: you're smart, you think quickly, and you have a good heart. And you smell like beef jerky."

"Why do you always remember my scent, grandma?"

"Oh, I remember everyone's smell, dear. Now, how about joining me for a game of Scrabb-Words?"

Bob heard a knock at the door. Without waiting for an answer, an orderly stepped in, carrying a syringe that would have scared the beard off Attila the Hun.

"Mr. Halibut, I'm afraid I'm going to have to ask you to leave," the orderly said, wiping his nose on his sleeve, "I need to give your grandmother her nightly painful injections."

Bob sighed. "Okay," he said, "Bye, grandma. I have some free time tomorrow afternoon, so I'll see you then."

"Just don't waste your night listening to that 'How to Enhance Your Relationships through Dialogue' CD again. Light off some fireworks or something."

"Edwina Halibut lived ninety long and blissful years. She always made time for her family, taking special care to write everyone in this room on a weekly basis. In her final years, she enjoyed caring for her fichus plant and listening to the musical stylings of Johnny Meatball and the Porkettes."

Bob hated funerals. He stroked his brown hair, combed for the first time in decades, and tugged at the shirt that imprisoned his portly form. Glancing around the room, he noticed all the relatives whose names he couldn't remember, the ornate church, the out-of-tune organ and the cornucopia of children squirming in their suits

4

and trying to pick their noses without getting caught. Grandma Edwina would've hated this. Way too depressing. There weren't even any cheese puffs on the refreshment table.

After listening to the eulogy, Bob stood by the refreshment table, stuffing himself with cheese and thickly-sliced ham. So entranced was he by the selection of meats and tiny buns that Bob barely noticed the figure walking toward him. The tall man had slicked-back hair, a slicked-back suit, and talked in a slicked-back way:

"Hi. Bob Halibut?" he said, jutting his outstretched hand into Bob's personal space.

"Yes?" Bob replied, shaking the hand warily.

"I'm Stan Powers, your grandmother's attorney. A sweet woman, your grandma Edwina was, you have my condolences, such a loss to the world, why do bad things happen to good people, blah, blah, blah. Anyway, I was wondering if you had time to discuss your grandmother's will. We have a lot of arrangements to make."

"Can it wait until after the funeral?"

"Ah, we can always put things off, Bob. But putting things off isn't a good code to live by. Just ask Neville Chamberlain. Now let's go somewhere quiet where we can discuss legal matters."

Mr. Powers tightened his grip on Bob's hand and, with a firm tug, led him to a small room. After shutting the door, he motioned to one of two chairs and whipped out a thin but heavily ink-stained piece of paper.

"This is your grandmother's will," he said, "As you know, she was a wealthy woman, and she wanted to leave—"

"I didn't know that."

"Oh. Well, she was. Anyway, her will is pretty simple. She told me explicitly she wanted to 'leave everything to Bob, who needs a serious kick in the pants, but is the only person I know with the gumption to use my money like I did.' She left you everything: her money, her car, her house-"

"I thought grandma sold her house before dad moved her into the nursing home."

"Not *that* house. The other house. You'll want to move in ASAP."

"Why's that?"

Mr. Powers raised his eyebrows. "Have you *seen* your grandma's house? Or her car? Or her boat? Or her plane?"

"Plane?!" Bob exclaimed.

Mr. Powers grinned. "You didn't know much about your grandmother at all, did you? You're going to have quite the weekend, Mr. Halibut."

Chapter 2

The house—actually it was more like a castle—was visible miles away, and as Bob pulled into the driveway, he was greeted by a fleet of classic cars. A huge cement fountain with a statue of Harry Belafonte juggling baby elephant seals sat in the middle of the circular driveway and an army of hedges (each sculpted into the likeness of a different chubby Malaysian prime minister) dotted the lawn. The place even smelled expensive.

Bob parked. Pushing with his shoulder, he opened the house's mammoth doors and walked into the main room. He wouldn't have been stunned by the house's exterior if he'd seen the inside first. It was extravagant, too, but it was…messy. Beneath the chandelier (which hung to one side and was broken in several places) lay huge piles of glimmering jewels and open treasure chests full of gold. In one corner was a pile of antique tapestries, and in another was a jade statue of a wide-eyed Chihuahua that seemed to stare into Bob's very soul. Stepping back, Bob slowly moved his eyes across the room again. There were beautiful paintings on the walls and giant rubies resting on pedestals and the creepy Chihuahua statue in the corner and pearls scattered across one side of the room and curious-looking bead necklaces and the creepy Chihuahua statue in the corner and mounds of coins of various metals and the creepy Chihuahua statue in the corner. Bob shuddered and covered the statue with one of the tapestries.

The only well-kept objects in the main room were the weapons; dozens of intricate swords, halberds, plasma rifles, laser pistols, axes, maces, and other implements of maiming hung neatly on the walls. Not a single speck of dust had dared to touch these treasures.

It wasn't until after several hours of exploring the house and discovering even more secrets that Bob heard his paunch of a stomach groan like a downtrodden goat. He strode into the kitchen but found it just as mysterious as the rest of the house. There was a table and a chair, but no fridge, sink, or microwave, and the oven wouldn't open no matter how much he pulled on the latch. Instead, the kitchen was full of strange holes in the wall which, upon closer examination, resembled headphone jacks. Bob was only a few minutes into his search for food when the doorbell rang.

He answered. It was a hairy, chubby man with a thick moustache and an orange shirt with a logo that had been obscured by years of sweat. He held a clipboard, and behind him were two muscular men carrying a wooden crate a little taller than they.

"You Bob Halibut?" the man asked.

"Yes."

"Sign here, please," the delivery guy said, handing Bob the clipboard. Bob signed and the man signaled his compatriots to carry the box into the house.

"What is it?" Bob asked.

"I don't know. Some lawyer—Powers, I think his name was—just told us to deliver it to you. Said it was from your dead grandma or something."

With a mighty thud, the delivery guys dropped the crate in the living room and handed Bob a crowbar. Bob tipped the three of them with gold coins and shut the door. Alone now, he stared at the crate, hesitant to open it.

Finally, he plunged the crowbar into the crate and pulled. The front of the crate snapped off and all four sides fell to the ground with a clatter. Bob dropped the crowbar. Before him stood a llama. A yellowish-brown llama with its eyes shut. It had a monocle on its right eye and wore a finely-pressed black suit and gray slacks. Like the house, the llama smelled expensive.

Then it stirred, opening its eyes and clearing its throat. It glanced around the house and shook its head. Disorder, as usual. The llama turned to Bob and spoke:

"Good afternoon, sir. The house is in a bit of disarray, wouldn't you say?"

Eyes wide as a baboon's buttocks, Bob took a step back. The llama took a step forward.

"I am Jeeves, your grandmother's butler. You've inherited me along with the rest of Edwina's possessions, and I dare say this

11

place is in desperate need of a good cleaning. Shall I start in the drawing room, sir?"

Bob just stared.

"I'll take your silence as a yes, then," Jeeves said. Trotting casually into the drawing room, Jeeves twitched his long llama neck slightly. A radar dish sprung from his forehead and began scanning the room. After a few seconds, it disappeared back into Jeeves' head as quickly as it had come.

"Just as I thought," Jeeves said, "millions of dust particles, carpet full of dirt fragments, box of silver coins 0.25 inches from its proper place, and trace amounts of cat feces. Edwina really left the place to rot while I was away!"

Bob crept closer to the finely-dressed llama, watching as a thick chord with a vacuum attachment on the end sprung from its midsection and began vacuuming the carpet. If it did notice him, the llama was not responding.

Swallowing, Bob finally worked up the nerve to speak: "What, uh…what are you?"

Jeeves paused. "I am a class-23 cyber-llama, programmed to serve your grandmother, Edwina Halibut. But I thought she'd have told you that."

"She didn't tell me much," Bob said, looking back at the kitchen.

Finished with the drawing room, Jeeves trotted bouncingly into the kitchen. Dozens of small wires shot from his sides and, like tiny tentacles, wriggled through the air until they found their way into the strange wall ports. The oven light turned on.

"Hmmm," Jeeves murmured, "Why don't you tell me what you do know about your grandmother?"

"Uh...well...she was born in 1926...had three brothers, one sister...studied Anthropology at Wellesley College...worked in a munitions factory during World War Two..."

"No, no, no! I mean, what do you know about who she really was? Her travels, her discoveries, her adventures."

"Adventures?"

Jeeves' cables flew out of the wall as the oven beeped and its door opened. Bending his long neck forward, Jeeves poked his head into the oven and recovered a golden-brown turkey. He gripped the hot pan in his mouth and set it on the table. Then he made an abrupt farting sound and, reaching behind him, produced a set of fine silverware.

"Yes, sir. Adventures," Jeeves continued, setting the silverware next to the turkey and motioning for Bob to sit down, "Your grandmother was quite the world traveler back in her day. I think I still have a few films of our travels in my data log if you care to see them."

"Great," Bob said, sitting down and cautiously examining his fork, "Why don't you, um, show them to me while I eat?"

"You'll need to access them yourself, sir," Jeeves answered, "Edwina was insistent that I store the videos in an inconspicuous place so that no unauthorized persons could access them. Just press the button in my left nostril."

Warily, Bob eased his finger into Jeeves' nose and heard a faint clicking noise. A bright light shot from the llama butler's eyes and projected a grainy, black-and-white image onto the kitchen wall. "This data log was taken on our trip to the Sahara," Jeeves explained, "It was after we recovered the Blue Ruby of Cairo from a local temple."

The woman shown was definitely Grandma Edwina, but she was young, beautiful, and more full of energy than Bob had ever seen anyone. She wore a leather jacket and cargo pants and ran as if possessed. Her arms swung by her sides as she ran and, in a pouch, she carried a large jewel.

Bob heard an engine revving. As the angle of the film's camera changed, Bob saw that Edwina was sprinting away from a black jeep while a deluge German curse words flew toward her. The young woman reached into her pocket and effortlessly tossed a grenade at the car, which exploded in a hail of fire and smoke.

The llama blinked heavily and a new image appeared on the wall. In this one, Edwina stood on a boat holding an intricate, golden statue. Arrows whizzed past her as she quickly knelt and fired a laser rifle at the opposite shoreline where dozens of half-naked islanders shrieked while reloading their bows.

"It's uncanny, sir," Jeeves chuckled, "Native peoples become so quarrelsome when you steal their war gods." He blinked again.

This new image showed Edwina surrounded by all sorts of wooden animals: rhinos, monkeys, beavers, hamsters, lions, huge snakes, and other creatures—each made of intricate gears, wires, bamboo poles, and wooden plates—swarmed Bob's grandmother as she desperately swung her polearm left and right. Lasers shot from beneath the camera, destroying many of the creatures.

"Here we are in combat with the wooden robo-creatures of Screaming Death Island," Jeeves explained, "My chest beams came in handy that day, I should tell you. Would you like to see more?"

"Yes," Bob found himself saying.

The old films continued playing and Bob saw his grandmother endure one deadly challenge after another; Through the images in Jeeves' eyes, she raced through ancient Aztec temples, battled vicious pirates on the high seas, and used a walrus to slide down a snowy hillside, pursued by spear-toting penguins.

Before he knew it, Bob had eaten almost the entire turkey. The images disappeared.

"That's all I have left in my data logs," Jeeves said, "Unfortunately, I had to delete some other films to make room for these. But I think you can see just a smidge of who your grandmother was now, can't you, sir?"

"Yeah," Bob said, shaking slightly as he came back into reality, "I had no idea. But...why did she do it, um...Jeeves, right?"

"Yes, sir."

"Why did she do it? The exploring and adventuring, I mean."

Jeeves put his hoof to his hairy llama chin and rolled his eyes up, thinking. "Well sir, she didn't keep me abreast of the reasons for her travels. I seem to recall the military hiring her a lot initially. To distract and perturb the Germans, you know. After the war, I believe she worked for different museums, historical societies, and anthropologists. There were the occasional secret missions funded by individuals with code names—I recall the two of us recovering a large cache of Atlantian gold for a Mr. 'Silver Banana'—her reasons varied.

"But if you were to ask for my opinion, sir, I would say she did it for the adventure. There wasn't a day your grandmother spent in this quiet, old house that she wouldn't rather have spent chasing after some ancient golden trinket or shooting at foes from the galley of a wooden warship. Being a cyber-llama, I'm not very good at reading human emotions, but I never saw more joy in your grandmother's face than when she was in deadly peril."

"I see," Bob said. He stood and began walking, slightly dazed, toward the bedroom. "Look Jeeves, it's been a long day and I have a lot to think over. I'm going to take a nap."

"Very good, sir," Jeeves said, "We shall discuss our first mission when you're more well-rested."

Bob ignored Jeeves' last comment. Falling on the gargantuan bed, he closed his eyes and was asleep in seconds.

When he awoke, he was surrounded by blackness. Bob guessed it was late, close to midnight. Rubbing his eyes, he stood and opened the bedroom door. In the doorway stood Jeeves, standing in the exact position he was when Bob went to bed.

"Are you quite rested, sir?" the llama asked.

"Yeah," Bob said.

"Good. Then we can discuss your first adventure. I'm quite looking forward to it."

"Wait, what?"

"Your first adventure, sir. Right before she put me into storage, Edwina explicitly told me that I was to conduct her successor to the pyramid of King Porkin Beanses to recover some of his lost—"

"You want me to go on one of these adventures?!"

"Of course, sir. Why do you think your grandmother left you all her possessions? It certainly wasn't so you could sit around and play Perturbed Birds all day or whatever it is you young people do these days."

"But—I—I just graduated from college. I've worked at Porkburger for two years. The closest thing I've ever had to an adventure was that time someone put tabasco sauce in my chocolate milkshake!"

"Well, you must start somewhere, sir. A journey to the pyramids would be just the thing to put a little spice in your life…instead of just in your beverage."

"But I could die!"

"With that attitude, sir? It's almost a certainty. Now, you'll want to bring along a fresh set of clothes and a few weapons, though you don't want to weight yourself down with—"

"But…I can't just run off! What'll I tell my boss?"

"How about 'I quit'? Might I remind you that you just inherited a gargantuan fortune, sir?"

"I'm no adventurer, Jeeves! No. No, I'm sorry. I'm not doing this."

Staggering back, Bob sat on the bed and stared at the wall, which held at a series of pictures of his grandmother in various exotic locations: Paris. Morocco. Tibet. He'd never even been to Montana.

Jeeves cantered into the room, sat down, and none-too-gently placed his hoof on the young man's back. "Master Bob," he said, changing his tone but not his expression, "Edwina loved you very much. Because you were family and her love was easily given. But her respect was not. I've only known you for a few hours and, frankly sir, I think you jittery, cowardly, a bit dull-witted, and rather pungent. But if Edwina thought you worthy to follow in her footsteps, I have full confidence in you."

He wasn't sure if Jeeves was technically a robot or not, but Bob saw sincerity in the llama's eyes. He thought about his job at Porkburger and his boring family and what surely awaited him if he stayed home.

Finally, Bob stood. "What weapons do you suggest?" he asked.

Jeeves chortled. "The scimitar is always a good, solid choice. It's a bit of a heavier weapon than the other swords. And you'll want a good laser pistol."

Chapter 3

Bob watched his wallet fade into the blue as the wind blasted past him. There wasn't anything left in his pockets, and the scimitar and laser pistol rattled erratically at his side. He gripped Jeeves' fur with all his strength, clenched his legs around the llama's sides, and clasped his eyes shut. Jeeves stood casually, his monocle unmoved, as his rectum rocket shot them through the air.

"Are you quite all right, sir?" Jeeves shouted.

"Yes," Bob said, swallowing quarts of vomit. Today wasn't a good day to wear one of his prized Hawaiian shirts.

"We'll be at the Nile Delta before long. One of your grandmother's old friends will greet us when we get there, and we'll travel to the pyramid tomorrow morning. Would you like some yogurt?"

Jeeves' storage compartment slid open and a small carton of strawberry yogurt, held firmly in place by metal clamps, rose toward Bob. He shook his head, and the yogurt returned to Jeeves' interior.

Just as he noticed they were over land, Bob felt a jolt as his llama butler halted. Jeeves lightly descended to the ground. When Bob finally opened his eyes, he saw that they were in the middle of a marketplace surrounded by a crowd of open-mouthed onlookers. Jeeves was expressionless.

After a few awkward moments, a fat, bearded man in a dark green tee shirt and disturbingly-short jean shorts came bounding toward them, waving his arms to dismiss the crowd. As soon as the people in the market had gone about their business, the man turned to Jeeves, a smile as big as his belly slapped on his face.

"Jeeves, my friend!" he cried, hugging the llama, "It has been a long time. I am sorry to hear about Edwina."

23

"Hello, Hamadi," Jeeves answered, "Yes, it surprised us all. But I do believe her tradition will continue. This is Edwina's grandson, Bob."

Hamadi shifted his bear hug to Bob's fragile frame. "It is wonderful to meet you, sir," he said, "I am Hamadi Chickennug. I ran messages for your grandmother when I was just a little boy, back in the '60s. Oh, I miss those days. Come! You stay at my house tonight!"

Hamadi's house was small, but homey, and Bob heard sounds of mirth and laughter on the inside. Hamadi ran up to the door and shouted:

"Wife! We are here!"

The door swung upon and a woman, at least as plump as Hamadi, gracefully walked toward them, a cascade of children around her knees. The children tackled their father and his guests to the ground. Bob sat up slowly among the swarm of little knees and elbows as the children clambered all over him, chattering so quickly that he wouldn't have understood them even if he had spoken Arabic. Hamadi whistled loudly.

The children climbed off Bob and gathered around their father. Hamadi cleared his throat. "Let me introduce to you my family," he said, pointing to the large woman, "This is my wife. I met her long ago during one of my missions for your grandmother, and we fell in love."

"Uh…what's her name?" Bob asked.

"Aziza," Hamadi answered, "And these are my forty-one children, Hanif, Acenath, Bebti, Frankie, Suzie, Johnny, Jack, Jill, Fred, Wilma, Gazoo, Terrance, Bungalo, Bertha, Doc, Happy, Dopey, Grumpy, Sneezy, Ebert, Kenneth, Rochelle, Dwalin, Balin, Bifor, Bofur, Bombour, Kielbasa, Crunchy, Chewy, Porker, Fettuccini, Quasar, Lumpy, Wilbur, Eggplant, Yolanda, Cockatoo, Sir Jefferson Hamsteak, Galactus Prime, and Ted."

Jeeves smiled. "You have a lovely family," he said, "I'm glad to see you're doing well."

"It is truly a wonderful life, thanks in no little part to Edwina. Come inside. We shall eat."

25

His greasy hands barely clutching the meat, Bob wolfed down his dinner of roast…whatever it was. It was tasty. And if he kept his mouth stuffed with food, he could avoid participating in the conversation any more than he had to. Hamadi and Jeeves ate leisurely while the children dug into their dinners like lions into emu.

"So your mission involves the Great Hives," Hamadi said, "I should have known. The incident with the Hives was one of the few times Edwina failed in her mission."

"Yes," Jeeves replied, "Most unpleasant, that one. We barely escaped with our lives. But then, that was in Edwina's later days. Bob is young and spry."

"That he is!" Hamadi laughed, giving Bob a hearty slap on the back. Bob involuntarily swallowed his meat.

"Has Jeeves told you of the hives, my friend?" Hamadi asked.

"No," Bob coughed, "He told me we were going to the pyramids."

26

"That you are. Most people know them as the 'pyramids.' Few know the truth."

Bob couldn't help but be intrigued. "The truth?"

Hamadi looked around cautiously and motioned to his wife. Nodding, she stood and closed the blinds. "Yes, the truth." Hamadi lowered his voice. "I know little of the pyramids' true nature, only what Edwina told me. But they hold a truly great treasure."

"Ancient treasures buried with the kings of Egypt, right?"

"No. Settle in, young Bob. I have a tale to tell:

"Long ago, Egypt was a peaceful farming community built around the Nile Delta. Life was simple, but happy, and went on much the same way for hundreds of years. Then came the hives.

"No one knows what they were or where they came from, but according to legend, huge diamond-shaped structures fell from the sky one day, embedding themselves in the sand. The exact contents of these hives is unknown, but they were suspected to contain some strange race of people from beyond the stars. And it was immediately after the hives came to Earth that the Egyptians rose to prominence as a world power, building structures and cultivating technology unknown in other parts of the world. Some think that the race of creatures that came in the hives—whatever they were—were conquered by the Egyptians, who used their technology and knowledge.

"The Egyptians recovered all the technology from top haves of the hives, the pieces visible aboveground— "

"The pyramids!" Bob exclaimed, trying and failing to mask his excitement.

"Yes," Hamadi continued, "But the lower halves of the hives remain hidden. For all we know, the lost race may live on still in the hives' bottoms."

"So we're going into the bottom hales of the pyramids?" Bob asked, scooting to the edge of his chair.

Hamadi smiled. "Edwina tried to get into the hives about thirty years ago. She nearly went in, but she did not wish to arouse…suspicion."

"What do you mean?"

"She had no idea what was down there. It could have been some sort of superweapon, and she didn't want it to fall into the wrong hands. The KGB was tailing her at the time."

"That's why she passed this mission on to you, sir," Jeeves said, gently dabbing his llama snout with a napkin, "We'll leave for the hives in the morning."

"But how will we get into the pyramids—hives, I mean?" Bob asked, "I assume they're pretty well-guarded."

"You just leave that to me and my family," Hamadi laughed.

Bob's air hole was small, and he sucked at it desperately, trying to breathe through the thick camel-hair blanket. He hung over Jeeves' back like a dead thing, disguised to fool the guards. Jeeves was being led by Hamadi, who strolled toward the pyramids, thirty-five of his forty-one children swarming around his legs.

The guard station in front of the pyramids was simple, but the guards were attentive and there were a lot of them. As he approached, Hamadi caught the eye of one particularly clean-cut guard.

Hamadi began speaking in Arabic. Through the blanket, Bob heard Jeeves' muffled whisper: "He's asking Hamadi what he's doing here and telling him that the pyramids are off-limits to visitors at the moment. Hamadi is explaining that he's travelled a great distance to show the pyramids to his children."

"Do you really think we should be whispering like this during a covert mission?" Bob asked.

"I assumed you'd want to know what they were saying, sir," Jeeves said, "Edwina always did. She said it made the adventure more complete."

The talking turned to shouting. Six of the Chickennug children had begun throwing hamsters at the guards. Bob heard their angry shouts amid the squeaky thuds of rodent hitting flesh and, through the air hole, spotted another contingent of guards sprinting toward the kids.

The remaining seven guards surrounded Hamadi, Jeeves, and the rest of the group. Bob heard more muffled Arabic shouting between Hamadi and the guard. Then there was an awkward silence.

"The guard just asked Hamadi what his children are attempting," Jeeves explained, no longer bothering to speak softly, "Hamadi told him that he needed to attract attention in order to get all the guards within range."

"Within range?"

"Yes." Jeeves shifted, letting the blanket roll to the ground and unravel. "You may want to watch this."

Hamadi closed his eyes and breathed in deeply. "Children," he shouted, "Attack formation 492!"

Like hyperactive centipedes, Hamadi's children began clambering on top of each other. The gaggle of guards lowered their weapons and just stood, mesmerized. Slowly, the cluster of youngsters grew larger and larger until thirty-five of Hamadi's forty-one offspring stood latched onto each other in one gargantuan child-sphere. Then the thing began to change form: a few of the children extended their bodies from the main clump, forming what looked like giant arms and fingers. Some of them lay

31

horizontally, forming feet, while those above them stiffened like huge legs. It was as if one huge being, made up of little children, towered above them.

Hamadi grinned. "I like to teach my children that, together, we are stronger."

The guards' mouths hung open. Before they had time to question their sanity, one of the fists made of youngsters shot out from the strange thing and punched a guard through the air. One of its child-legs sprang forward and kicked another, thrusting him back. With a swift punch, the mechanized child-beast knocked out the remaining guards.

Bob heard pounding footsteps. More guards were coming. Digging in its heels, the monstrosity of children extended its arm. With a bang, it fired children through the air one-at-a-time like tiny missiles, bashing the approaching guards. Hamadi dashed forward to stand with his children.

"Go, my friends!" he shouted, pointing to the pyramid entrance, "We'll hold them off!"

Grabbing the shocked Bob, Jeeves tossed his master onto his back and ran inside the dark, musty door of the largest pyramid. It wasn't long before the sights and sounds of the raging skirmish faded into the blackness. With a short click, Jeeves' retina floodlights kicked on.

The wonder of the pyramid's huge stone interior struck Bob like a cold, wet pair of tighty-whities. All around him were carved stones, indecipherable hieroglyphics, and enormous statues of people long forgotten. Most of the ancient kings' treasures had been cleaned out, but the engravings of ancient gods – Ra, Set, and one that looked like Fred Savage – stared at Bob like a brooding squirrel at one who would steal its nuts.

Bob remained lost in his own mind until he heard a slam. The stone door had shut and, in a flash, the dark pyramid was illuminated. Jeeves remained unmoved. He was gazing at a pedestal that sat between two sculptures. They looked similar to the other statues, but on their heads were wide, majestic afros, and they wore garments the llama had never seen in any book on Egyptian history. On the pedestal sat an emerald.

"A most interesting stone, don't you think, sir?" Jeeves commented.

Bob turned to his llama. "Uh…I guess."

"Why don't you take it?"

Bob thought for a moment and shook his head. "The government would have taken that jewel along with the rest of the treasure years ago, especially since it's right by the entrance," he reasoned, "It's probably connected to a booby trap or something."

"Oh, there's no doubt about that, sir. A booby trap, no question."

"Then why did you want me to take it?"

"Because adventures aren't nearly as fun if you don't spring all the booby traps. Otherwise, how are you to manage a daring escape?"

Bob gave Jeeves a stare before he spoke again. "No thanks, Jeeves. I think I'll do just fine without the impending death."

"Very well, sir. I'll take it."

34

Before Bob could react, a mechanical arm snaked out from Jeeves' back and plucked the green stone from its perch. With a thunderous blast, a booming voice sounded from out of nowhere:

"Who dares to seize the Emerald of Naughtiness?!"

"Bob Halibut does, dear sir," Jeeves answered.

"Then prepare to taste death, one called Bob Halibut!"

The ground quaked. As Bob glanced wildly around him, he felt a hand clutch his ankle. He kicked it away. Bob saw more and more hands spring from the pyramid floor and, after gripping the cold stone, begin to pull up the decayed bodies attached to them. Horrible, gray creatures that used to be people heaved themselves up, groaning. As soon as they yanked their crackling bodies from the cracks in the ground, they began shambling toward the pair of adventurers.

Without conscious will, Bob drew his scimitar and laser pistol and walked backward until his derriere touched a stone wall. He stood, side by side with Jeeves, filled with more adrenaline now than he had been in all his life. As the creatures drew closer, Bob noticed that, though the bodies of his opponents were ancient

35

and decayed, their clothes looked modern: they wore sequins, bracelets, hoop earrings, and bell bottoms. Their hair was also strangely well-kept and many of them sported afros identical to those on the statue. They moved now in strange patterns, all in unison.

"What are they doing?" Bob asked, turning to his llama and trying to hide his fear.

"Dancing, sir," Jeeves answered, "the undead are always a bit behind the times, I'm afraid. Honestly, who dresses like that anymore?"

Bob tried and failed to swallow the lump in his throat. "Jeeves," he asked again, "what exactly are we facing?"

Jeeves' face hardened. "Disco zombies, sir."

Chapter 4

Bob tightened his grip on the sword. He hoped Jeeves would take point and shield him from most of the disco zombies. The llama did no such thing, and the funky-fresh corpses continued to shamble forward. Sweat pooled on Bob's forehead. Finally, not knowing what else to do, he bellowed like a savage John Goodman and charged, firing his laser pistol like a madman.

Though he wasted an entire energy magazine, Bob had managed to drop two zombies. Shrieking, a nearby zombie clawed at him. With instincts he didn't know he had, Bob dove out of the way and swung his scimitar, chopping off his foe's decayed head. The varied dance moves of the dead were difficult to dodge, but

Bob kept on his toes, slashing everywhere. He was terrified. And it was the greatest feeling ever.

Jeeves casually strode forward, coming closer and closer to the menacing dancers. Finally in range, he opened his mouth, activating his flamethrower. A gout of fire engulfed several zombies, who were soon nothing more than piles of ash in shiny clothes. Anchoring himself using his front legs, Jeeves spun to the right, promptly kicking two zombies' heads off with his hind hooves.

"Don't feel sorry for the living dead, sir," he said, "They don't feel pain. But didn't I tell you? Adventuring is in your blood."

Bob didn't hear his butler. One of the zombies had entangled his blade with a large gold chain, and Bob thrust his enemy's weapon to the ground, blasting the creature in the chest. Two came at him from either side. Bob punched one in the face and slashed the other in half. Pushing forward as one mob now, the zombies tried to crowd him. Bob leapt back, whirling his sword around his head. He panted furiously.

The zombies abruptly stopped advancing and Bob heard the booming voice again:

"You fight well, Bob Halibut. I shall have to alter the field of battle."

With a slow scraping, the stones that made up the top of the pyramid slid back. Bob stared upward as a house-sized, spherical object descended from above. A mirror ball! The pyramid grew dark once again, and the ancient ball rotated, slowly at first; but it soon filled the room with spinning flecks of light. Colors flashed across the sand-covered stone and, as if commanded by the gods themselves, the ancient sounds of the Bee Gees blared.

The zombies began moving again and Bob steadied himself, raising his scimitar. Out of the corner of his eye, he caught a sight that made him retch: a severed arm digging its fingers and elbow into the sands and inching along all by itself. Legs, arms, and heads squirmed along the floor and meticulously began to stitch themselves back together. Every zombie Bob and Jeeves had taken down was reforming.

Jeeves turned to his master, whose nostrils had grown wide with fear. "Now would be a good time to reload, sir," he said.

He was getting used to the weight of the curved sword now. With two mighty strikes, Bob shattered a few zombies, but his arms were beginning to ache and the monsters' bodies soon stitched the holes Bob had hewn. He looked to Jeeves, who had produced a lace handkerchief and was wiping his monocle.

"How do we destroy them?" Bob shouted.

Jeeves thought for a minute as he kicked through a zombie ribcage. "It seems to me, sir," he said at last, "That if we cannot take them down one-by-one, a precision strike is in order.

"What do you mean?" Bob yelled, slashing at a few zombie claws drawing uncomfortably close to his face.

"Hold them off, sir," the llama said, blasting his lasers into the throng of zombies. "I need to concentrate."

Snapping a fresh energy magazine into his laser pistol, Bob steadied his aim and, more carefully this time, began firing. Six zombies dropped. Taking a step forward, Bob swung the sword and fired in the opposite direction. As he cleared a path through the advancing horde, one zombie hopped in front of Bob and, squatting slightly, began swinging its clenched fists up and down. It was doing the monkey! The top of the creature's fist hit the scimitar's pommel and knocked the sword from Bob's hands.

His laser pistol clicked. Bob tried to reload as the zombies closed in, but soon found himself punching and elbowing his attackers. A claw ripped at his shirt, and Bob could feel the decayed breath on his face, the smell of millennia spent without toothpaste nearly overpowering him. Flinging his empty pistol a few feet away, Bob cracked a zombie's skull with his fist. A dozen of the rotting creatures surrounded him now, grasping and clawing in every direction.

A loud clang echoed throughout the pyramid. Bob's eyes shot up to see the disco ball falling toward him like a tumbling boulder. Using a concentrated stream of laser vision, Jeeves had severed the tie between the mirror ball and the ceiling. As it neared he and the zombies, Bob saw how large the ball really was.

Bob reached behind him and grasped an unfortunate zombie by the shoulders. Kneeling like a coiled spring, Bob jumped, still clasping the zombie. He flung it upward in an arc and, arms still throbbing, positioned himself underneath it. The zombie smashed through the glass, creating a hole in the mirror ball, which Bob deftly slipped through.

No sooner was he inside the giant sphere of mirrors than the ball smashed against the stone of the pyramid floor, shattering into huge fragments. The disco zombies were crushed, slashed apart, and otherwise destroyed. Still in midair, Bob desperately tried to evade the massive glass shards from inside what used to be the mirror ball, dodging and kicking. He yowled as one sliced his arm and another nicked him on the cheek.

Soon, he hit the floor. Bob clutched his stomach and stood. The music had stopped and the zombies were no longer reconstructing themselves. Jeeves casually floated down from the ceiling, holding the emerald high and gleaming.

"Nicely done, sir," he commented, "You're more ingenuitive than I first thought."

"Why did you grab that emerald?!" Bob yelled, staring at the green stone, "You could have killed me!"

"But I didn't, did I? Now, come along. I suspect we must travel further into the hive to find the treasures we seek."

"Uh…how do we do that?"

"I imagine it has something to do with this emerald, sir. Otherwise, it wouldn't have been so heavily-protected."

Jeeves' body tensed and his head began rotating around the room. He froze and hopped a little.

"What is it?" Bob asked.

"My sensors have located a slot in the wall, sir. It's the exact size of the jewel. Putting this gem into its proper hole may open a path into the rest of the pyramid."

"Or it could set off another trap."

"It's probable. But I think we could use another adrenaline rush, don't you?"

Bob didn't answer. Cautiously, he set the jewel in the wall's slot. With a click, the emerald slid into place and the wall began to rumble. Ancient stones ground against each other as the wall moved upward, the dust of thousands of years sliding onto the stone floor. Before him was a dark passageway, and the stench of emptiness greeted him from the blackness. Once again, a voice thundered from the beyond, knocking Bob to his knees:

"Do you really wish to delve further into my hive, Bob Halibut? The dancers were just the beginning. I have other ways to expel you from my crypt. Be gone and leave me to my eternal rest!"

Jeeves paused but seemed confused rather than afraid. He trotted into the passage suspiciously.

"Should we leave?" Bob asked, though he already knew the answer, "I mean, it's been fun, but I wouldn't want to suffer the legendary curse of King Porkin Beanses."

"Sir," Jeeves said, adjusting his monocle, "that is no ancient pharaoh. If that voice really belonged to Porkin Beanses, why would it have referred the pyramid as a 'hive?' And do you not find it suspicious that this ancient Egyptian temple speaks English? There's something strange going on, sir. Our duty is to find out what it is.

Jeeves' eyes lit up once again and he cantered into the hallway fearlessly. As they explored the passage, Jeeves' gaze

44

drifted to the ground. He halted and held out his hoof, blocking Bob's way forward.

"What is it?" Bob said.

"These floor stones are different from the others," Jeeves replied. Gingerly, he pressed one of the stones with his hoof. Bob heard a loud twang, and a small dart appeared in the wall. Extending his mechanical arm, Jeeves plucked the dart from the wall and examined it.

"It's tipped with an odd chemical," he explained, staring at the dart intently as his sensory systems scanned it, "and the floor is covered with pressure plates that cause the darts to shoot from the walls."

"Just like in *Raiders*."

"I suppose if movies are your only frame of reference, than yes; this is similar." After another few seconds of examination, Jeeves' usually calm and squishy face contorted into a look of shock.

"What is it?" Bob asked, "Is it tipped with poison?"

"Hardly," Jeeves answered, dropping the tiny projectile, "The ends of these darts are coated with a lethal ancient laxative."

"A laxative?"

"An archaic Egyptian substance known as Anubis-Lax. Even a tiny dose causes one to *completely* lose control of one's bowels. If you get hit with one of these, your sphincter will pry itself open and your body will evacuate all its vital organs out of your rectal cavity. A most gruesome way to die, if I do say so myself."

Bob thought for a moment. "But, you can fly, can't you?"

"I can, sir," Jeeves answered, "but I'm afraid the force of my rectum rocket would upset the delicate pressure plates. I believe my hoof spikes may be a better solution."

Jeeves rose off the ground a few inches, sharp spikes now jutting from his hooves. Trotting up the walls, Jeeves soon stood on the ceiling and looked down at his master.

"Great," Bob said, "So I can just cling to your back while you walk across?"

"No, sir. Our combined weight may be too much for the hoof spikes. You'll have to climb across on your own."

"What?!"

"The ceiling stones are ancient, sir. There are quite a few crevices and notches you could use for handholds."

"But what if I lose my grip and fall?"

"Then you'll be stuck by about twenty laxative-laced darts. I'd rather not think about what would happen afterward."

Bob shook his head and clambered up the wall until he clung desperately to the ceiling. As Jeeves sauntered quickly to the other side of the hallway, Bob cautiously stretched out his arm and grabbed what he hoped was another crack in the stones. It was. Little by little, he crawled across the ceiling, trying and failing not to look at the deadly pressurized stones below and the tiny holes on either side of the hall. With every inch gained, Bob felt more strongly the tension from the spring-loaded darts that waited to pierce his flesh.

A sudden pain shot through Bob's middle finger as he stuck his arm into another crack in the ceiling. Bob yanked his hand out of the hole and flailed it around wildly, trying to shake off the rat that had latched on. Before he realized what he was doing, Bob had flung the rodent off his finger. He watched as it fell, almost in slow motion, to the floor and compressed one of the tiles.

Bob didn't have time to think. Tensing his legs, he leapt forward, away from the spot where the rat had fallen, and began to drop. He heard the whizzing darts behind him as, somersaulting, he prepared to hit the flat stones. Instinctively, he drew his sword. As soon as he hit the pressurized rocks, he leapt again, desperately trying to stay ahead of the dart spray like a grasshopper fleeing from a bullfrog. He thrashed his sword around wildly, the loud ping of the darts telling him he'd deflected certain death.

Just before he hit the hallway floor again, Bob felt something grip his shirt and yank him forward. Jeeves set Bob back on his feet and retracted his mechanical arm as he inspected his master.

"Amazing, sir," the llama said, "I don't see a single dart. It seems you have your grandmother's spirit in you after all."

"Thanks," Bob said, "Is that the end of the death traps?"

"It's hard to say, sir, but I'd guess we're pretty close to our destination. Look behind you."

Bob glanced into the next room and saw a series of walls with intricate hieroglyphics sketched into them. Everything from a great battle with humanoid crocodiles to a fall harvest to a yak milking a ferret was depicted on these walls. The dust and sand here weren't as thick as they were in the rest of the temple, and this room, more than any of the others, felt cold and empty.

"We've reached the center," Jeeves explained, "If Edwina's theories are accurate, the entrance to the lower half of the hive should be around here somewhere. Tell me, sir, what do you think of the wall decorations? "

Bob pawed at his chin. "They seem a little excessive," he said, "almost as if someone were trying to hide something."

The small radar dish sprung from Jeeves' head, and he scanned the room. "There," he said, pointing to a dark corner, "If my mechanical innards are correct—and they are—something in that area should lead us to the rest of the hive."

After an awkward silence, Bob realized Jeeves expected him to inspect the corner. Creeping forward, he was relieved to find no booby traps. Squinting at the hieroglyphs, Bob spotted a tiny, circular segment that jutted out from the rest of the wall...a button? Trembling a bit, Bob pressed the device.

With a rumble, a segment of the floor began to move, and Bob heard the grating of stone against stone as, gradually, the ancient rocks slithered back, revealing a hidden staircase. The stairs, untouched by man, sharply contrasted with the rest of the pyramid; they had no dust or wear at all and seemed more metal than stone. At the end of the stairway was a faint, purplish glow. And if he listened closely, Bob could hear high-pitched, otherworldly noises coming from the lower floor. He looked to his llama.

"Well? What are you waiting for?" Jeeves asked.

Sword still drawn, Bob gingerly descended the stairs and turned the corner. He beheld a cave, stadium-sized at least. The silver walls glimmered under the light of the huge purple crystal in room's center. Everywhere, high-tech devices—Bob couldn't begin to guess what they were—hummed and buzzed. There were machines that looked like car-sized, floating green cubes linked together with a series of tubes and others piled in a corner that resembled giant, bronze potatoes with bicycle seats attached. Large devices, gadgets that resembled chrome motorcycles without wheels, lined the walls. The taller contraptions were surrounded by tiny, metal scaffolding. But Bob was most astonished by the cavern's inhabitants.

They were guinea pigs. Dozens of chubby rodents scurried around the room, using a variety of alien tools to work on their machines and squeaking to each other in a dialect not heard by humans in centuries. Each wore a different human-style hat, perfectly-sized for their guinea pig head. Bob froze as he gazed at the fedoras, fezes, akubras, balmorals, pith helmets, shakos, sombreros, monteras, gats, and dozens of other pieces of headgear.

As he marveled at the undiscovered wonders of the past, Bob heard a tiny squeak at his feet.

He looked down. There stood a guinea pig, taller than the rest, wearing a handsome top hat. Though he had never seen these creatures before, Bob could sense this guinea pig's regal air.

"Greetings, human," the portly rodent said, removing the cigar from its mouth, "And welcome to our hive."

Chapter 5

Bob didn't know if what struck him was wonder or fear or a little of both, but it prevented him from moving. The guinea pig scurried toward Jeeves.

"Well," Jeeves said, raising his eyebrows, "This is a fortuitous turn of events. My name is Jeeves and this is my master, Robert Halibut. We'd heard rumors there were undiscovered wonders in the lower halves of the hives. But I never expected anything like this."

"You have my congratulations," the guinea pig replied. "We've seen neither human nor llama in centuries. I am Mr. Squishy. Please, let me show you around."

Bob followed the skittering guinea pig, careful not to step on the other little furballs that scampered around him. Gradually, the guineas dropped their work and crowded around the newcomers' ankles, chittering excitedly. As they journeyed deeper into the rodents' underground home, Bob spied tiny, thatched huts with mud roofs, out-of-place next to the machines, he thought.

"We do not pay much heed to material comforts," Mr. Squishy explained, noticing Bob's curiosity, "Our focus is the creation of new technology. As you can see, we are currently building new vehicles and creating more efficient ways to generate energy. That purple crystal you saw earlier radiates enough power to sustain one of your cities for five-hundred years. Oh, and by the way, take this with my compliments."

From beneath his hat, Mr. Squishy produced a small vial of blue liquid, which he tossed to Bob.

"What's this?" Bob asked.

"The cure for the common cold. We've had quite a bit of time to research disease, being isolated underground for so long."

"But why haven't any humans discovered your civilization until now?"

"Uh…we've arrived!"

Bob, Jeeves, and their guinea pig entourage stood before a golden structure, big by Bob's standards but enormous to the rodents. Six towers stretched to the hive's roof, and tiny bricks of gold fit tightly together to form each one. Intricate carvings that resembled Egyptian hieroglyphics decorated the edifice and four-foot statues of heroic guinea pigs wielding swords, axes, and spatulas and wearing magnificent hats lined the walkway.

The palace (for that was what it was) did not house the same kind of wondrous technology as the rest of the tiny mammals' homeworld. It had many windows, large and small, but only one parapet, which held a tiny leather recliner that faced outward. Two well-dressed guineas with curved horns stepped onto the parapet and trumpeted their instruments loudly. They shouted something to the assembled crowd and all the rodents fell prostrate.

"The great, powerful, and irresistibly-attractive Pharaoh Porcellus graces us with his presence," Mr. Squishy whispered hastily, "Strangers, bow before the almighty one, whose bellybutton lint is more beautiful than a thousand sunrises!"

Bob didn't appreciate the command, but dropped to one knee. Waving his arms regally, a particularly-chubby guinea pig sauntered onto the parapet and plopped down in the recliner, forcefully pulling the chair's lever and elevating his feet. His tiny whiskers were crusty, coated in ice cream and marmalade and other kingly delights. A golden headdress like those worn by Egyptian pharaohs rested on his head and his eyes were locked on Bob with an expression of intrigue and caution.

Letting out a single squeak, Pharaoh Porcellus raised his paw, and all the assembled guineas leapt up. In a voice both high-pitched and booming, he spoke in the ancient guinea pig tongue.

"The great Pharaoh Porcellus, whose armpit sweat is sweeter than the finest wine, welcomes you to our home," Mr. Squeaky translated, "and asks if you will join him in the courtyard for a feast. He has much to discuss with you."

"Well..." Bob stuttered, still staring into the Pharaoh's piercing eyes.

"We'd be delighted," Jeeves chimed in, "Please give the Pharaoh our thanks."

The feast consisted of lots of cheese, goat, food pellets, nuts, beef jerky, and shimmering silver goblets full of grape soda, all spread on a table about as big as Bob's sword. The Pharaoh sat at one end with some of his fez-wearing officials, and Bob, Jeeves, and Mr. Squishy at the other. Despite its size, the courtyard was beautiful; tiny fruit trees and bushes flourished and the sound of a fountain filled Bob with sense of tranquility. Pinching his tiny utensils and stabbing at the tiny food, Bob was surprised when, at Pharaoh Porcellus' command, servants scurried into the courtyard carrying human-sized forks.

The Pharaoh squeaked boisterously as he dug his fangs into a large piece of jerky.

"The all-seeing Pharaoh Porcellus, whose voice is akin to that of Frank Sinatra gargling unicorn tears, asks how you came upon our realm," Mr. Squishy explained.

"We are...explorers," Jeeves said, "who heard the legends of your hives and wished to see your great civilization for ourselves. We have traveled far and faced many dangers to find your city."

Pharaoh Porcellus took another gulp from his goblet and let out a few more squeaks. "The Pharaoh, whose dandruff is the table salt of the gods, wishes to know more of human civilization; tell the great one of your technology."

There was a lull in the conversation. "I believe the Pharaoh would like an answer from the human," Jeeves explained.

"Oh," Bob said, "Well, our technology has advanced quite a bit since you last interacted with humanity. We have gasoline-powered vehicles called automobiles that transport us more quickly than any horse. We have electronic boxes called televisions that broadcast images over great distances. We even have vehicles capable of travelling into outer space—"

"And what of your weapons?" Mr. Squishy interrupted, "What of your military technology?"

"Um…well, we mostly use firearms. We also have tanks and artillery units that fire large rounds, aircraft, missiles—"

The Pharaoh squeaked again. "What kind of missiles?" Mr. Squishy asked.

"I'm not sure. I'm not really a weapons expert."

"I see," Mr. Squishy said, "Then let us talk of other things. How do you like our city? It's been ages—literally ages—since we've had human visitors. I hope you will stay for at least a few days."

"Yes," Jeeves replied, "Your way of life is growing more fascinating by the minute…"

The purple light of the lower hive made it hard to sleep and, as he tussled on the thick cot, Bob tried to calm himself and slumber. The bustle of the guinea pig colony had faded away, and all had returned to their thatched huts. Bob told himself it was the excitement of discovering an ancient civilization that kept him from sleep. But as he lay there, fifty feet from the palace, he could feel Pharaoh Porcellus' eyes glaring through him like a pair of those obnoxious blue headlights through the darkness.

At last, Bob stood, deciding to take another look at the creatures' colony. The machines, untouched, slowly hummed as they awaited the day. If he listened closely, Bob could hear tiny snores echoing through the silver cave. He tried to take his mind off his worries by examining the machines once more, but felt himself drawn to the palace and, gradually, made his way to the golden castle. From the top of one of the towers, Bob spotted a tiny beam of light.

With all the stealth he could muster, he crawled. An eeriness crept down his spine as he heard the squeaking of the Pharaoh. Though there was no darkness here, the palace looked different at night. Instead of its splendorous towers and golden hue, Bob now noticed the strong gate, closed tight, and the unwelcoming stone wall that surrounded the courtyard. There were also quite a few guards, more than surrounded the castle during the day. They hadn't spotted him yet. Bob took another step.

Then he stopped. He heard a new sound: footsteps. Behind him. Frozen, Bob slowly reached toward his hip, and his hand came to rest on his gun. Swallowing hard, he whirled around, drawing the laser pistol and taking quick aim.

"Well, it's good to see you too, sir," Jeeves whispered.

Bob lowered his pistol and relaxed his shoulders as the llama hushed his voice even more.

"I see I wasn't the only one unable to sleep," Jeeves said, "nor the only one on-edge."

"Yeah," Bob replied, "I don't know why, but I have a bad feeling about the Pharaoh. He certainly didn't seem happy to see us."

"Yes, and I thought it odd that the guinea pigs had an English interpreter and human-sized utensils prepared for us when they didn't know of our coming. And the Pharaoh seemed far too interested in human military technology. Let's look in on our dear Pharaoh."

"But what about the guards?"

Jeeves turned to the east side of the palace. For a moment, he just stood. A few clicks and buzzes pierced the silence as a dozen tiny turrets sprung from his midsection and fired tiny darts. With nary a sound, the guards dropped.

"After all these years, my precision targeting system still works like a charm," he said, cocking his head, "Never doubt cyber-llama engineering, my dear boy."

Though he could easily peer into the upper chamber, Bob was cautious as he glanced through the window. There was Pharaoh Porcellus in all his plump glory, pacing around the room and muttering something in his ancient language. The room was ornately decorated with golden statues, bejeweled mirrors, and a microphone labeled "scary pyramid voice." But the first object to catch Bob's eye was a stone tablet. It was covered in etchings and, occasionally, the Pharaoh would glace at it, sneering.

Bob could barely make out the pictures on the tiny stone. Toward the top was an image of a guinea pig, the sun's rays behind it, sitting atop an Egyptian palace. Humans surrounded this small rodent, bowing. The next pictograph depicted a guinea pig, arms outstretched, tossing cylindrical objects into the air. These were gladly received by the rejoicing humans. Such pictures covered the stone, showing happy guinea pigs, humans, and these curious cylinders.

Then, on the lower portion of the tablet, the pictures began to tell a different story. They showed the furred visitors gladly eating the cylinders, while the humans sat, hungry, shaking their fists at their rodent companions. A large carving toward the tablet's bottom displayed an enormous battle between human and guinea pig. The chubby rodents seemed to be defending their cylindrical treasures from the human attackers. Bob thought the final image pretty graphic, even for a stone carving: the humans danced in their victory, consuming their precious cylinder items with relish, while the few surviving guineas crawled agonizingly toward the pyramids. It was this final image that made the Pharaoh scowl with seething anger.

After what seemed a fortnight, the door to the pharaoh's chambers flew open. At the top of the staircase stood a guinea pig in a dark, maroon robe tied with a yellow cord. His face was hidden, but he held a bright, purple gem, similar to the large one that towered over the furred animals' domain. A grin spread across the pharaoh's fuzzy face. The other guinea pig spoke in a deep tone and walked to the table, setting the jewel down. Porcellus' rubbed his paws together.

The robed rodent raised his own paws high and recited an ancient chant. Though he couldn't understand the rodent, Bob was chilled by its words. As the guinea pig droned on, the jewel glowed brighter and brighter until both Bob and the Pharaoh shielded their eyes. A faint whine came from the gem and it began to shake. With a force that almost knocked the table over, a beam of energy shot out of the purple stone and rocketed across the village.

Bob and Jeeves, knocked to the ground by surprise, couldn't tell where the robed guinea pig had aimed the beam. But it didn't take them long to find out. The purple glow of the guinea pig homeworld grew brighter. Just as the smaller gem had, the gigantic crystal became more and more dazzling; the smaller stone was feeding energy into the purple crystal at the cave's center.

When this jewel, too, grew almost white and began trembling, it shot its own beam into the air. The sound was deafening. Rodents sprinted from their huts, shrieking, as the beam blasted through the ceiling of their home and through the roof of the pyramid itself. For the first time in thousands of years, the sun's rays pierced the guinea pigs' cavernous home and the tiny creatures gathered at the palace, their hearts ablaze.

As quickly as they had started, the horrible sights and sounds stopped. The crystal returned to its normal state. The chattering guinea pigs were greeted by their Pharaoh, whose head shot from the tower window.

His loud squeaking echoed throughout the cave. As the guinea pigs looked to their leader, their expressions turned from fear to happiness and, soon, all were cheering. Spying Mr. Squishy amid the crowd, Bob and Jeeves pushed through the guineas toward the translator.

"What did the Pharaoh just say?" Bob yelled over the squeals of celebration.

"The all-knowing Pharaoh Porcellus, whose flatulence is sweeter than the most costly perfumes, says that he has given the signal to our guinea brethren. We attack now!"

"Attack who?" Bob asked. Jeeves nudged Bob and subtly glanced at his weapons. Bob gripped the hilt of his sword.

With a gaze full of spite, Mr. Squishy and many of the other guinea pigs unsheathed weapons, both old and new. Spears, swords, axes, laser guns, and otherworldly metallic staffs glinted in the silver light.

"You and your kind," Mr. Squishy answered, "We have suffered under your rule long enough."

The furred animals encircled them, and Bob and Jeeves stepped closer together until they stood back-to-back."

"But why?" Bob asked, drawing his laser pistol and scimitar.

Mr. Squishy sighed, his grave, serious eyes full of sadness.

"For the churros," he said, "We must retake the churros."

Chapter 6

The world grew dark. In an instant, something hard smacked Bob across the eyes, there was a bright flash, and the guinea pigs fell on their tiny keisters. He turned to Jeeves.

"Flash bulb, sir," Jeeves explained, "I thought I'd better cover your eyes before I launched it. Shall we be off?"

Bob leapt on his llama. Jeeves' rectum rocket blasted its fiery payload, and the two sped toward the stairway to the human world.

It didn't take long for the tiny warriors to recover from the flash. Bob heard furious little shouts as laser bolts whizzed past them. They were far from the bulk of the guinea pigs, but many dotted the path between Bob and the stairway. Smoothly, Bob whipped his sword back and forth on either side of Jeeves, smacking the guinea pigs away and cutting a swath through the rodents.

With a kick, Jeeves sent one of the guinea pigs flying. As his sword grew heavy, Bob spotted something near the top of the silver cave. Guineas in sleek, black suits slid down from the dark corners of the ancient structure, their tiny halberds hungry for human flesh. These seasoned fighters dropped expertly onto Jeeves' back and surrounded Bob.

He tried to slash them with his scimitar, but they were too close. Tiny claws dug into Bob's shoulder as one of the vermin clambered up and thrust its halberd straight at Bob's eye; he leaned back just before his face was skewered. Another swung at Bob's ribcage. He dodged, but the blade nicked his arm, bringing with it a spurt of blood. A third guinea stabbed downward, gouging Jeeves' right rear leg.

The llama let out a brief yelp and quickly regained his composure. "Sir," Jeeves said, his voice strained, "I'm going to attempt to dislodge these rodents. Grip my fur tightly."

68

Bob did so. Still flying at top speed, Jeeves began spinning like an eggbeater. The attacking guinea pigs flew off in all directions (as did Bob's stomach.) Soon, Jeeves had leveled out again and, it appeared, had left the guinea pigs behind him. The stairway was in sight.

From atop his litter, carried by jogging, panting servants, Pharaoh Porcellus squealed with rage. Mr. Squishy was soon by his pharaoh's side.

"Mighty pharaoh, whose dead skin flakes are more delicate than the petals of the lily, fear not. The human and his companion have outrun our guards, yes. But they still must contend with Smoochykins."

The pharaoh stopped yelling and smiled, sinister joy coursing through his veins. He squeaked the order, and Mr. Squishy produced a teeny remote control.

Jeeves twisted sharply around the corner and rocketed up the stairway. Fortunately, the entrance to the guinea pigs' lair was still open, and he and his master were soon in the entrance room where they had seen the strange hieroglyphics. Jeeves jerked to a stop.

"Why did you stop?!" Bob shouted, "They're still behind us!"

"We must proceed on foot from here, sir," Jeeves replied, "Do you not remember the dart-shooting hallway?"

Bob nodded and they walked briskly toward the deadly corridor. A great stone slab plunged from the ceiling, landing between the entry room and the hallway and blocking their way out.

"Bollox!" Jeeves said, "They've sealed us in!"

"What do we do now?" Bob cried.

"I suggest making things right with God, sir."

As they waited for the guinea pigs to descend upon them, Bob felt the ground tremble. It went still, then shook again. A series of booming sounds was coming from the darker areas of the huge room. And they were getting closer. Bob spotted a pair of glowing red eyes in the darkness and heard a great, bellowing squeak. Into the light stepped a guinea pig, tall as an evergreen tree, wearing thick, spiked battle armor. In its paws was a sword nearly as large as Bob and a round shield with a crest of crossed churros emblazoned upon it. It stood erect, glaring at the intruders.

"Well, that's a bit of bad luck, isn't it sir?" Jeeves said, "I'll see if I can't dislodge this nasty rock in front of the dart hallway. Why don't you handle this nuisance?"

"Why me?" Bob demanded, just noticing the blood stains on the gargantuan creature's lips.

"Because you're the adventurer, of course. It wouldn't be much of an adventure if I helped out too much, would it?"

The mighty guinea pig arced its sword downward, and Bob, who sprang out of the way just in time, watched in horror as the pyramid's stone floor splintered before the weapon. The guinea pig took a step forward, swinging its shield and smacking Bob in the face. Tasting blood, Bob flew across the room and smacked into the opposite wall.

As he stood, Bob whipped out his laser pistol and fired. He heard a ping as the blast bounced harmlessly off the battle armor. The giant rodent smiled and licked its whiskery lips. Snarling, it charged forward. Bob's eyes darted around the chamber. His weapons couldn't match this rodent's. Not knowing what else to do, Bob gripped a loose slab of stone and, sweating and grunting like a woman in labor, hefted it above his head. His arms quivered and ached, but he looked determinedly at his foe.

Just before the roaring rodent rogue was upon him, Bob heaved the stone. There was a loud crack as it struck the guinea pig squarely in the face. With a screech of pain, the beast stumbled back. Bob glanced at Jeeves, who was slowly melting the stone that blocked the hallway with his laser vision.

"Good show, sir," Jeeves said, "But you'll need to hold him off a bit longer. I'm almost through."

In seconds, the guinea recovered and was hollering curses in its ancient guinea pig tongue. Throwing its shield aside, it gripped its sword with both paws, held it aloft and thundered toward Bob once again.

"We don't have 'a bit longer,'" Bob stuttered, looking from Jeeves to the guinea pig and back again.

Bob sidestepped until he was just behind Jeeves. The guinea pig changed its course, bawling all the louder as it prepared to cleave the human in two. Just as the rodent finally reached its quarry and leapt toward the pair of adventurers, bloodlust seeping from every pore, Bob hopped to the side, slamming against Jeeves.

The two flew out of the guinea pig's path, and the giant rodent slammed into the stone blocking the hallway. A crash reverberated through the chamber as the stone shattered before the force of the guinea pig, who fell, still shouting, to the floor. Dashing out of the room, Bob and Jeeves jumped over the monster and stopped abruptly. Before them was the corridor of laxative-tipped darts.

Rubbing its bruised head, the guinea pig grunted. Once it regained its bearings, it bit down on the sword, clenching it between its massive incisors, and charged on all fours.

"Bravo, sir," Jeeves said, "We're trapped between an oversized, psychotic rodent and a hallway that promises to doom us to a fate I'd rather not envision. You are Edwina's grandson, there's no doubt."

"Now's not the time for sarcasm!"

"That wasn't sarcasm, sir. I'm fascinated. Bold escapes were Edwina's specialty. I can't imagine what you'll do to get us out of this."

"Uh…right. Because I have a plan."

Adrenaline flooded Bob's mind. The guinea pig's eyes were fixed on him like a laser, and cold beats of sweat formed on his brow. Almost without thinking, Bob spotted the leather straps holding the guinea pig's armor on its body.

"Jeeves!" he cried, "Shoot its armor straps and grab the plates!"

Obediently, Jeeves fired several laser blasts, expertly snipping the chords that bound the breastplate and back armor to the guinea pig's torso. As soon as they were cut, Jeeves' mechanical arm, like a striking cobra, snatched the two metal plates.

To Bob's relief, he found that if he knelt down slightly, one of the plates completely covered one side of his body. He handed one to Jeeves.

"Hold it on your left side," he explained, "And crouch a bit so none of your skin is exposed to the darts. I'll hold mine on my right. Make sure you match my speed."

Jeeves positioned his armor plate as he had been instructed. "Now what, sir?" he asked.

"Run," Bob said, glancing back at the beast closing in, "Now."

The twosome trotted briskly. As soon as they set foot in the hallway, the darts began to ricochet off the armor, but the plates held sturdy. Bob found it a little difficult to keep pace with Jeeves, who cantered just as he always did, while the deadly darts pelted the metal mercilessly. They had moved only a few feet before the giant guinea pig came storming down the hallway after them.

A legion of soft thuds told Bob that the darts had found their mark. The guinea pig tumbled, squeaking heavily. Without a word, Bob and Jeeves quickened their pace; both wanted to be as far from the monstrous rodent as possible when the darts' chemicals took effect.

As they entered the upper room at the front of the pyramid, Jeeves plucked the emerald from its slot in the wall, and the stone door leading to the hallway descended. Bob sighed with relief.

"It's not over yet, sir," Jeeves said, "We must get out of this place and warn everyone."

"Warn them about what?" Bob asked, still panting.

"Just before they attacked, sir, Mr. Squishy mentioned something about the rodents' 'guinea brethren.' I fear they may have agents in the human population."

To Bob's surprise, the door to the outside easily slid open. With his cyber llama in tow, Bob ran into the sunlight. The pyramid guards jumped, spilling their playing cards and bags of potato chips everywhere, and leapt to their feet. Bob felt sweat collect on his face as the guards drew their weapons. But he soon had other concerns.

The ground quavered. The guards began shouting in Arabic once again. Bob heard the foundations of the pyramid crack as they rose from the earth they'd been planted in for millennia, sand cascading off the huge stones. Slowly, the great hive rose and revealed its underside, which like the guinea pigs' home, was silver and shimmered in the sun's rays like the surface of a lake. The guards, speechless, watched helplessly as the gargantuan diamond rose and floated high above the earth.

With a deafening grinding, the ancient stones began moving. Rock slid against rock as sections of the mammoth diamond slid past each other, changing the hive's shape entirely. It got longer and thinner and at the front. Many of the stones simply fell away, revealing a glass pane...a window? On the structure's sides, stone panels slid up and revealed steel cannons with glittering buttons and lights, and at the back, a colossal hole formed. Soon the stones were all in place. Fire shot from the rear opening and the craft rocketed forward, leaving a gust of sand in its wake.

"It's as I suspected," Jeeves said grimly, "Their mothership has taken to the skies."

"Mothership?!" Bob exclaimed.

"Indeed, sir," Jeeves said, crouching a bit and leaning toward Bob, "Hop on."

"What?"

"Hop on, sir. We must pursue."

The rectum rocket fired and they were airborne. Acid swelled up in Bob's stomach as his cold sweat caught the wind and chilled him to the core. He drew his sword.

Chapter 7

Bob felt the force of the wind against his face subside as he bent closer to Jeeves' fur. He opened his watering eyes. Though they were still far from the guinea craft, Bob could spot the hovercycles he'd seen in the guinea pigs' lair. Like a thousand screaming birds, a barrage of green laser bolts streamed from the alien vessels. Jeeves weaved expertly between the bolts.

"They're drawing closer, sir," Jeeves observed, "And the closer they get, the more deadly their aim becomes. My laser vision isn't very accurate at this range. We'll have to use something else."

The fur just below Jeeves' neck parted, revealing a control panel. Dozens of flashing lights surrounded the buttons, switches, and screens that showed Bob the view from every angle of Jeeves' body.

"Might I suggest a heat-seeker, sir?" Jeeves said.

"Uh…which button do I press to launch it?" Bob asked.

"Oh, of course. You haven't read my operator's manual. Well then, just start pressing buttons and flipping switches. You'll find something useful eventually, I'm sure. Just mind the self-destruct switch."

"Which one is that?"

"The red one."

"Which red one?!"

"Uh…just start flipping them, sir. I'm sure our luck will hold."

His gaze still on the laser fire, Bob pressed a large, purple button. Jeeves' body jolted and began to shake. Bob braced himself. With a ping, a panel in Jeeves' side popped open and a metallic cupholder thrust a glass of orange liquid toward Bob.

"What's that?"

"Carrot juice, sir. You activated my juicer. You should drink it. It's quite good for your eyesight."

A laser bolt whizzed by and singed the hair on Bob's calf. He flipped another switch. The metallic panels beneath Jeeves' chest slid outward one-by-one, revealing a cannon. The recoil made the cybernetic llama halt briefly as it fired, shooting a basketball-sized lump of white...something...at the guinea pigs. The chunky-looking missile smashed through one of the hovercycles' engines, sending it careening toward the ground as its pilot's guinea pig curses filled the air.

Jeeves smiled. "A rather unconventional use of the mashed potato cannon, sir, but I enjoyed it."

The green bolts of energy were everywhere now, scorching Bob's skin like the heat from a campfire. Squirming to keep his balance on the zigzagging llama, he began pushing buttons and flipping switches like a sugar-addled toddler with a new toy lawn mower. Finally, after activating a bubble gun, a crayon sharpener, a weasel launcher, satellite TV, and a surprisingly pleasurable buttock massage feature (in that order), Bob pressed a button that opened Jeeves' stomach panels. Two long, multi-barreled cannons covered in flashing scopes, laser ammunition belts, and other

81

paraphernalia too fantastic for the movies rose from Jeeves' stomach cavity and locked into place, one resting on each side. A heavenly chorus of rock music played in Bob's head as a large joystick with an even larger trigger popped from Jeeves' neck.

Trembling, Bob squeezed the trigger. The cannon on Jeeves' left whined as a ball of fiery blue energy built up at the gun's muzzle and, in an instant, blasted off to meet Bob's furry foes. The weapon on Jeeves' right, a rusty, gray cannon with a barrel covered in round holes, chattered as it rained its laser payload down on the guinea pigs. The four nearest hovercycles became balls of metal and fire.

Jeeves banked to the right to dodge a laser blast. The rest of the guinea pig cycles had arrived and now surrounded Jeeves, swirling around the llama like dozens of giant, silver wasps. Bob clenched the trigger. The posh llama dashed and darted wildly and, rather than depending on his rider to aim, angled himself so as to draw the cycles into his master's line of fire.

"They're out of effective cannon range now, sir," Jeeves commented, trying to take Bob's attention away from the joystick,

"I believe some sword work would not be out of place, if you can manage it." Bob nodded.

Jeeves jerked upward, dodging another laser blast and arcing just over one of the guinea craft; Bob thrust his sword down, stabbing into the flying machine and shattering the engine. But his white-knuckled left hand still gripped the firing mechanism. The crack of laser fire covered all other sounds and the heat of the rapid fire cannon, just a few inches away from Bob's leg, felt like a second sun.

Spotting movement to his left, Bob lashed out with his sword, smacking a rodent pilot with the flat of the blade and sending it squealing into the distance. Some of the blue energy from Jeeves' laser cannon began flicking his thick fur, sending the smell of burnt llama rearward.

"Let go of the firing mechanism, sir!" Jeeves shouted as his rear hooves bashed the engines of another guinea craft, "They're too close now!" Bob released the trigger, his shuddering hand still in a claw-shape. The swarm of hovercycles grew larger, nearly entrapping the two companions in a giant, silver sphere of cycles.

One such craft drew closer and closer to Jeeves' rear. The hovercycle was nearly invisible amid the throng, and the target was far too busy dealing with the other vessels to notice. The pudgy rodent aviator smirked, sinister glee burning in his fuzzy belly. He slowed his cycle, bringing the engines to a soft hum, and crept toward his prey, thinking of the churros of legend and of the humans' cruelty. He steadied his craft and readied his trigger finger.

A thunderous smash broke the hum of hovercycle engines. Jeeves whirled around in time for he and his master to see the metal shards of a guinea pig cycle—one they'd missed—fly in all directions. Something had shot from the ground and shattered the craft. Bob squinted to see through the smoke and finally made out…a child?

The little girl smiled, gave Bob a thumbs up, and dropped just as quickly as she had bolted upward. Bob spotted another explosion and heard another child squeal with joy as guinea cycle shrapnel burst from another destroyed vehicle. The panicked animals broke formation as more and more youngsters rocketed into the sky and tore through their vehicles. It put to shame any fireworks show Bob had ever seen.

The radio housed in Jeeves' ear, which Bob hadn't noticed until now, began crackling, and a familiar voice laughed and cheered:

"Good to see you again, my friends! It appears we found more than we bargained for beneath the pyramid, eh? You seemed overwhelmed, so we thought we'd give you a hand."

Jeeves motioned for Bob to look down. Far beneath them was a rusty, red pickup truck. Bob could barely make out the details, but it appeared to have a large cannon made of PVC pipe resting in the bed and surrounded by a legion of giggling children. The airborne children, their faces blackened with guinea pig hovercycle exhaust, plummeted like fleshy missiles. As they came closer to the ground, each calmly pulled on their shirt collar. Metal poles popped from the backs of their shirts and colorful, Dacron wings jutted out, creating miniature hang gliders. Angling their bodies to catch the wind just so, each of the children soared back to the vehicle and landed softly in the truck bed, ready for another turn in the cannon.

Jeeves laughed. "Your children are even more skilled than you, Hamadi!" he shouted into the radio, "I can't believe it's been so long since our last escapade."

"It is good to be adventuring again, my ungulate friend. But there is no time to talk; the children have cleared a path."

Most of the hovercycles had either fled or exploded and Jeeves, setting his rectum rocket to maximum thrust, careened toward the mothership. Bob's muscles tensed as they closed in on the transformed pyramid, but surprisingly, no weapons appeared. The flying llama drew nearer to the huge vessel, and as the ship's jagged, sandstone exterior came into view, tiny cones sprouted from the ship's surface and flew toward Jeeves. Missiles!

Jeeves craned his neck and faced his master. "Sir," he said, "I'm afraid if I try to dodge those missiles or deploy countermeasures, we'll sacrifice too much speed and lose the ship. You'll have to go in on foot."

"What?!"

"Take this radio," Jeeves continued as a small, plastic rectangle popped out of a compartment in his back, "And try to find that purple crystal. I have a feeling that stone is the key to the guineas' plans."

"But how am I going to get inside the pyramid?"

"By rolling to absorb the impact of the landing, sir."

Cutting all power to his rocket, Jeeves stopped abruptly. Like a rock from a slingshot, Bob flew forward, flailing and screaming. The guinea pig vessel seemed to rush toward him as his feet scrambled to find solid ground and came up with nothing. Remembering Jeeves' instructions at the last moment, Bob tucked his arms into his body and bashed against the stone roof of the pyramid ship, rolling and bouncing until at last he landed on his back, in pain but unbroken.

The rushing wind made it difficult to stand. The roar of the engines was deafening, and the ship's surface quaked as Bob searched for a way inside the vessel. His search was not long. A submarine-like hatch popped open and a tall guinea pig strode onto the ship's exterior. Despite the torrential wind, its tophat stayed perched on its head, and it carried a tiny rapier. The pudgy creature strode steadily toward Bob until it stood a few feet away.

"The arrogance of you humans astounds me," Mr. Squishy said, brandishing his sword, "We came to this planet in peace. But your ancestors proved the falsest of friends."

Like a spring, Mr. Squishy leapt, swinging his rapier madly. Bob barely deflected it with his own blade.

"We shared our technology with you, but you squandered it and claimed it as your own!"

He jumped again, striking with two quick slashes. Bob took a step back, parrying one of the attacks and just dodging the other. The steel scraped his shoulder, and he felt a sharp pain.

"We even shared with you our churros! Our lifeblood! The sugary gift of our forefathers!"

Mr. Squishy knelt and swiped at Bob's legs. Bob jumped over the sword strike, but staggered when his feet touched the vessel's surface. He hadn't realized how uneven the ship was; the roof sloped down from the center, creating a sort of rounded tent shape.

"And you slaughtered us! In your churro-lust, you put our ancestors to the sword!"

Bob deflected Mr. Squishy's blows as best he could, occasionally glancing at his feet. The ferocity of the enraged guinea's attacks gradually drove him back, toward the ship's edge.

"Now we rise and take what's ours! Already my guinea brethren all over the world begin to respond to our signal! And once we have conquered your race of churro thieves, we shall rain our fiery vengeance—"

Bob saw his opening. As soon as Mr. Squishy's sword no longer covered his belly, Bob punted the chubby rodent. For a moment, Mr. Squishy bounced across the ship like a rubber ball, but he soon leapt back to his feet, his tophat still clinging to his teeny head.

The guinea pig sprinted. Fumbling, Bob drew his laser pistol and fired, but Mr. Squishy swung his rapier and deflected the shot. Hopping above his opponent, Squishy thrust his sword down as Bob sidestepped. He tried to slash Mr. Squishy across the belly, but the furry ball of fury deflected the strike and stabbed wildly in Bob's direction.

It was difficult to focus on anything but the squealing terror before him, but as Bob parried and evaded Mr. Squishy's blade, the occasional scrape making him wince, he studied his environment. Particles of sand still flew from the ancient stones, and the flames of the ship's booster licked the sky with gouts of fire. Mustering his courage, Bob let out a shout. It didn't sound quite as fierce as he would have liked it to, but it made Mr. Squishy jump back a bit. Dashing forward, Bob whipped his sword in all directions until it seemed nothing but a silver blur. He clenched his eyes shut and, one belligerent step at a time, herded his opponent backward.

A swift bite from the guinea's sword made Bob's fingers release his weapon. Immediately, Mr. Squishy stepped on Bob's blade and leveled his own at the human. Panting, he grinned.

As he said a silent prayer, Bob swept his legs out from beneath him and dropped to his back, kicking his right leg at the guinea pig. Hit squarely in the stomach, Mr. Squishy released his

rapier and shot back like a tennis ball from a serving machine.

Back he flew, off the rear edge of the ship. With one last, desperate

squeal, he vanished.

Bob picked up his own sword and ran toward the hatch.

Jumping through the round opening, Bob landed inside the ship,

knees bent and weapons at the ready.

Chapter 8

Just like the inside of the pyramid, the ship's interior was dry and musty. Bob stared down the corridor before him. Even through the thick stones, Bob heard the bustling and squeaking of the guinea pigs scrambling to enact their plans. Clenching his weapons, Bob crept down the hallway until at last he came to a corner. A green light peeked around the bend and the jittering rodent voices grew louder.

Bob's sweaty finger slid to his laser pistol's trigger, but he soon thought of the attention a laser blast would attract and turned the pistol around, grasping it by the barrel. Standing flat against the wall, Bob sucked in air as quietly as he could while the guinea pigs stepped into the open. Two tiny laser rifles were hooked to their backs, and each had a peculiar device, something that looked like an oversized watch, strapped around its waist. The guinea pigs chittered noisily, and though he knew not what they said, Bob sensed the malice in their squeaking.

One of them, a fat, gray creature wearing a ten-gallon hat, paused. It raised its paw, signaling for its companion to be silent. The foul rodent's nostrils billowed delicately, and Bob's weapons became slick as a thin layer of sweat formed on his palms. The pig with the cowboy hat began craning its neck around, eyes inching toward the intruder, as it reached for its laser rifle.

Bob arced his weapons downward and struck with the butt of his laser pistol and the pommel of his sword. With a thud, the steel of his weapons hit the backs of the guinea pigs' diminutive heads. They let out not a squeak.

Once Bob was sure the rodents were knocked out, he uncoupled one of the watch-looking devices. Like the rest of the guinea pigs' equipment, it was a bright silver and, like a digital watch, had a large, circular screen and buttons on the side. Pink symbols, prehistoric guinea pig script, flashed across the screen.

Bob pressed one of the buttons and another image appeared: a video recording of Pharaoh Porcellus barking out instructions as he munched on a cheese poof. Bob pressed another button. More guinea pig script. Frantically, he fiddled with the watch, scrolling through indecipherable glyphs, otherworldly images, and a disturbing video featuring a walrus covered in lime gelatin. There had to be something here he could use.

At last, the screen displayed a pink, web-like structure. At the center was a purple diamond and the pink strands branched out from it like vines. They looked like...passageways? This was a map. And the prominence of the purple diamond told Bob that Jeeves was right; the purple crystal was the epicenter of this craft.

Moving quickly but cautiously through the hallways, Bob glanced from the device to the halls and back again as he tried to pinpoint his location. He grabbed his radio.

"Jeeves," he said in a hard whisper, "Are you there?"

"Absoloutely, sir," Jeeves answered in a normal tone, "Are you inside?"

"Yeah. You were right about the crystal. I think it's powering the ship."

"I fear it's doing far more than that, sir."

"Why? What's going on out there?"

"We have a slight…problem."

"What do you mean 'problem?'"

"Well I'm not sure about your definition, sir, but I believe hundreds of guinea pigs with laser rifles streaming across the desert sands clearly constitutes a 'problem.'"

"What?!"

"It would seem the pharaoh has been planning this little escapade for some time. You'd best hurry, sir."

Weaving around corners like a buttered serpent, Bob finally came to a circular room. Purple light streamed from the doorway, and Bob could see the shadows of guinea pigs skitter around the command center. He strode forward, cursing the sound of his footsteps as his feet grated against the stone.

As he took another step, Bob heard a click as the stone beneath him sank mechanically. The echoes of the guinea pig chatter ceased. With a sharp blast, a blaring alarm siren sounded and, as Bob pawed at his ears, the room began to quake. All around him, stones rose and began to twist and flex, changing shape like dough. Rumbling as they awoke, the stones on the floor, the ceiling, and the walls grew long and cylindrical and slid into position. Bob stood, still rubbing his ears, and was promptly bashed on the chin by a five-foot stone tentacle. He fell to his back.

Rolling to his left, Bob dodged another tentacle, which thrust down from the ceiling and jabbed into the floor, spraying gravel. Bob jumped up, but another rock tentacle smashed into the space between his eyes. Flecks of blood spurted from his mouth. Bob bolted for the door, bounding out of the way of one stone arm and ducking beneath another.

Something jerked his ankle. With a cry, Bob fell, face first, onto the ship's floor. He dug his fingernails into the stone beneath him, trying to crawl away, but the tentacle's grip on his foot didn't loosen. Another of the stone things, snaking almost playfully from its place in the wall, shot forward, aiming for the heart.

Bob swerved, swaying his body to the left. The tentacle scraped by, tearing his shirt, and Bob felt the cold of the primal stone as it flew past his exposed belly. The tentacle continued its path forward; with a crack, it crashed into the tentacle gripping Bob's leg, smashing it and freeing the young adventurer. A jolt of pain shot through his contorted foot. As best he could, Bob once again bolted for the doorway. He was closer now to the room bathed in the purple light of the crystal and could make out the shapes of the guinea pigs inside more clearly. He drew his gun.

Rock coiled around both of Bob's wrists, jerking his arms upward and outward, and both his feet were soon ensnared, too. Rising and pulling his limbs taught, four stone tentacles held Bob upright. And they kept pulling.

A stretching pain crept through Bob's arms and legs as the tentacles continued to pull. Bob stared forward determinedly. Popping sounds sprung from his arms. He squinted.

Though his vision was beginning to blur, Bob singled out the silhouette of a tall guinea pig wearing a maroon robe and holding a long staff and squeaking some sort of chant. His hand trembling as he contorted his wrist, he aimed the laser pistol.

Bob's shot hit its mark. The sorcerer flew backward, smacking into the chamber's floor, knocked unconscious. Bereft of the enchantment, the rock tentacles released Bob and slithered back into the stone. With his arm still outstretched and his finger still on the laser weapon's trigger, Bob grit his teeth and staggered into the command chamber.

The crystal stood on a pedestal in the room's center, and Bob felt warmth emanating from the antique gem. Behind the crystal was a viewscreen straight out of *Trek Wars* surrounded by dozens of tiny workstations, each with a guinea pig typing away furiously. The room was adorned with shimmering crystals of every color Bob could have imagined, thousands of black wires latched onto buzzing engines, and weapons. Hundreds of ornate swords, spears, axes, chain maces, regular maces, daggers, pikes, bows, halberds, flails, whips, and javelins hung from practically every surface like fingerpaintings on the wall of a preschool. A tapestry depicting a disturbingly-muscular version of Pharaoh Porcellus hung behind the bejeweled golden throne where the pharaoh himself sat, nibbling on a green jelly bean.

A barrage of crackling sounds came from the guinea pigs' computers. The viewscreen depicted several suburban homes, where dozens of pet guinea pigs leapt from their cages and assaulted their human masters. As the image of a guinea pig attacking an elderly woman with a salad fork burned itself into his mind, Bob lowered his laser pistol in disbelief. Time was short; the worldwide guinea pig revolution had begun.

Almost simultaneously, around thirty rodents whirled away from their computer screens and stared at the young adventurer. Shivering, Bob once again raised his pistol as the vermin scampered toward him from all sides of the room, squealing their war chants wildly as they drew their energy rifles. He gritted his teeth. Just before the tiny troopers fired their miniscule weapons, an eardrum-shattering squeak blasted from the throne. The guinea pigs glanced at their pharaoh, who slid off of his throne. Glaring at the human, Pharaoh Porcellus waved his paw. Confused, the guinea warriors chittered softly, but at a loud squalk from their leader, they scattered.

Porcellus just glowered at Bob for a moment, his petite eyes radiating hate. Like a conductor, the guinea pharaoh raised his arms and, as mystic wind rushed through his red-brown fur, floated. Bob heard the clattering of metal against stone. As Porcellus' gaze hardened, the weapons popped from their wall mounts and glided to the middle of the room. Bob gripped his laser pistol tight as hundreds of hovering blades stared back at him.

Chapter 9

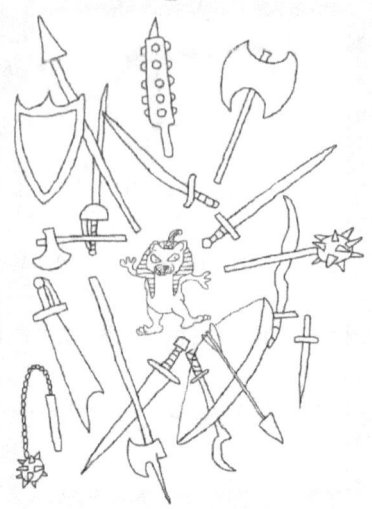

Porcellus smirked as, with a flick of his paw, the floating weapons flew at his opponent, surrounding Bob in a windstorm of blades. But the guinea pig pharaoh knew better than to savor the moment for too long. Dozens of sharp, blunt, and otherwise painful metal implements flung themselves at Bob. Darting to the left, Bob parried a flying rapier with his own sword; he ducked as a dagger whizzed overhead. Running like a thing possessed, he swerved to avoid a chain mace and leapt over a javelin, which nicked his heel.

A longbow and a leather quiver filled with arrows floated majestically, but speedily, down from the ceiling. As if guided by invisible arms, an arrow rose from the quiver and knocked itself.

The bowstring bent, and the arrow shot toward Bob like an angry hornet. He was able to hop out of the way, but a second arrow soon came his way. Like a monkey trying to dodge rain, Bob goose-stepped through the chamber, arrows cascading all around him.

He made a dash for the middle of the command center, where Porcellus floated, giggling. Raising his blade to deflect the quiver's final arrow, Bob drew his laser pistol and fired at the guinea pig tyrant. Instantly, a wall of shields clumped together in front of Porcellus and the blast bounced off harmlessly. The shields bolted away from Porcellus as quickly as they had come, and the pharaoh squeaked something in his ancient tongue that sounded like prehistoric mockery.

At Porcellus' command, a lance streaked toward Bob. Reflexively, Bob jumped onto one of the guinea pig-sized computer terminals, pivoted, and then leapt again, hopping over the lance like a hurdle-jumper and pushing it down with his palm. It crunched into the stone floor. Bob kept running, only a few yards from Porcellus now.

His sweaty finger almost sliding off his laser pistol, Bob fired again. Porcellus raised a shield to deflect the shot. Bob eluded a swinging tomahawk and let another blast fly. Porcellus raised a shield to deflect it. The guinea pig hovered in front of Bob at eye-level, though Bob knew he had the power to float higher. But he didn't. This was a taunt. Raising his scimitar, Bob mustered his energy and charged, leaping at the rodent king and arcing his sword at its furry head.

A falchion flew between Bob and Porcellus and parried the human's blow. Bob spotted a longsword flying toward him. Snatching it out of the air, he struck with his scimitar, swinging at Porcellus with both swords. But a flurry of whirling blades continued to block his blows. Out of desperation, Bob thrust his elbow forward, but a studded shield shot up to parry it. His arm hit the shield with a bang and, as he shouted and clenched his aching arm, the shield clattered to the stone floor.

Barely dodging the battle axe that swung for his neck, Bob dropped onto his back, snatching the fallen shield as he rolled. Springing up again, he thrust the shield forward and bashed the rodent's whiskery face. Porcellus darted away, screaming as he clutched his forehead and clenched his eyes. He'd moved out of sword-range again; Bob's tactics were getting him nowhere. Glancing once again at the horde of weapons, which still drifted menacingly around the room, Bob decided to hide.

He sprinted to the pharaoh's throne and ducked behind it. Though it had been built for a guinea pig, the throne was far larger than the pharaoh, and Bob was (barely) able to conceal himself. He wheezed heavily but, he hoped, not loudly, as the guinea pig monarch's mocking squeaks stung his ears.

Flipping patties at Porkburger suddenly seemed like a Caribbean vacation. Bob beset his mind for a way to defeat the devilish rodent. Peeking out from the throne's edge, he watched Porcellus float casually around the room, arms crossed, as he grew angrier by the second. Metal whipped around the guinea pig, protecting him from every angle. Sighing, Bob stared angrily at his useless scimitar and shield.

The shield that, only moments ago, Porcellus had wielded effortlessly with his magic. Bob thought back to the lance he had sent clattering to the floor and the longsword he had snatched from the air, and a question ignited his mind: why hadn't Porcellus used his own weapons against him? The rodent king could have used his mystic energy to wrench Bob's scimitar from his hands, leaving him defenseless. Unless he couldn't. Unless any weapons that touched human flesh were immune to the pharaoh's magic.

Porcellus had his back turned to the throne now. He was floating directly between Bob's line of sight and the purple crystal powering the ship. The bow that had plagued Bob earlier was hovering nearby, just out of reach. He tightened his grip on the scimitar.

Bounding out from behind the throne, Bob jumped and grabbed the bow, dropping to one knee as he hit the stone floor. He prayed he could keep his hands steady as he balanced his sword's pommel on the bowstring, pulled back with all his might, and lined up his shot.

With a twang, the sword soared from the bow, honing in on its target like a hawk. Porcellus whipped around as he heard the whine of the airborne blade, but he was too late. The scimitar rammed through Porcellus' Egyptian-style crown and continued on its path, embedding itself deep in the crystal.

The flying weapons froze. Then, all at once, they fell to the floor with a clang, along with Porcellus, who hit the floor with thud. The bright, purple glow that had once enveloped the entire room faded as cracks began to wind through the crystal. The pharaoh let out a high-pitched, gurgly cough. With a final, hateful squeal, he closed his eyes as he lost consciousness. Bob lowered the bow and began to breathe again. For the first time since he'd entered the command chamber, he felt the pain return to his arms and ankle and legs. But as he limped through the layer of weapons strewn across the stone floor, he couldn't help but grin.

A crack reverberated through the room. Bob turned and saw the crystal lean more and more to the left, until at last it fell from its perch.

The room shook. The blades on the floor rattled wildly as stones broke from the walls. Bob bolted for the chamber door, falling stone crashing all around him. After a mad dash through the room where he had fought the stone tentacles, he came to the narrow hallways of the pyramid ship and darted around like a rat in a maze. He drew out the navigation device, but all that met him was a blank screen.

Stumbling, Bob felt the floor shift beneath him. The balls of his feet rose with the rock, and he tried desperately to stand, clutching his ankle. The ship was reverting back to its original shape! The sound of fracturing stone grew closer. He crawled, climbing the floor through a hallway he hoped would lead him to the exit.

A handful of pebbles dribbled onto Bob's head, and he heard something heavy shift above him. A sandstone brick plummeted from the ceiling and split over Bob's noggin, turning everything black.

Bob awoke to the smell of beef, beans, dates, and Play Dough. The thick, wool blanket was making him sweat like a schnauzer on the equator, and his head felt like a giraffe had just tap-danced on it. He sat up and pried his eyes open, blinking the sleep out of them. His vision was blurry, but he could make out

Jeeves, a chubby man and woman sitting at a table, a crackling television, and lots of tiny figures. As soon as they saw him rise, about fifteen of these figures tackled him, giggling.

"He is awake!" Hamadi laughed, "I knew the blood loss wouldn't do him in! You owe me fifty pounds."

"Oh, alright," Jeeves sighed, reaching into one of his many fur-pockets for his wallet.

"What happened?" Bob wheezed as the children's combined weight pressed down on his chest.

"You won, sir," said Jeeves, "Well done."

The smell of Play Dough was much stronger now and it jogged Bob's memory. "But the guinea pigs," he stammered, "Their ship—"

"It crash-landed in Beni Suef shortly after I pulled you out, sir. And I dare say the authorities will be scratching their heads over this one for some time."

Bob winced as a little knee dug into his ribcage. "But all over the world, the guinea pigs are revolting."

"Actually, we've been watching the news and it seems the rodent revolution has come to an end. Guinea pigs are a funny species, sir. Without a leader, they're slow to act, and that crystal you destroyed seems to have been restoring the intelligence the surface-dwelling guinea pigs lost over the millennia. I don't think they'll be bothering us for some time."

"But what about—"

"Sir, come here and eat."

Dozens of little hands dragged Bob from the bed and set him at the table. The beef and beans were a welcome sight, and he ate ravenously.

Hamadi chuckled. "It is like Edwina always said: adventures make the mind full but the belly empty. Or something like that. Let's eat."

As the sun dipped beneath the horizon, Bob bathed for the first time in days, said goodnight to Hamadi's forty-one children (one-by-one), and sat in the glow of a crackling fire, sipping coffee with Jeeves, Hamadi, and Aziza. The desert heat had gone, and a cool wind stroked their backs through the open window.

"This is what I miss," Hamadi said, draping his arm over Aziza, "Sitting around a fire with a good friend and a pungent llama. I haven't done this in decades, but it hasn't really changed."

"Indeed," said Jeeves as his robotic arm lifted the coffee to his llama lips.

"What are you two going to do now?" Aziza asked.

Bob looked at Jeeves. "I'm not sure, actually," the cyber llama said, "This trip was the last adventure Edwina planned before she grew too old for the whole thing and had me packed away. I suppose we can stay with you for a bit."

"Actually, that was not what we had in mind" Aziza said, turning to her husband, "Show him, dear."

Hamadi shifted and reached inside his shirt pocket. "A few days ago, just after you told me of your coming, I looked through my old chest. I keep souvenirs from old adventures in there: ancient trinkets, old weapons, expired fruit leather, you know. And while I was digging through my old treasures, I came across this.

Hamadi produced a yellowed, rolled-up piece of parchment, which he handed to Bob. Dust drizzled off the scroll, and it stunk of age. The antique writing was surprisingly clear. In the firelight, Bob could make out a circle with intricate pathways, elaborate doors, and mysterious symbols drawn inside it. At the center of it all was a book with a ray of light streaming from it.

"What's this?" Bob asked.

"I remember discussing it with Edwina once, but she did not say much. As I recall, she told me it was a map of an Aztec temple somewhere in southern Mexico." Hamadi grinned. "But she just called it a 'treasure map.'"

Jeeves nudged his master. "Well, sir, what do you say?" he asked, "Are you ready for another mission?"

Bob swallowed. "Uh...I think I'd like to go home for a while, actually. And take a rest."

"Of course," Jeeves said, "What was I thinking? We'll have to wait until your gaping head wound is mostly healed before we go on another adventure. And we'll need a little time to prepare. You'll have to choose another weapon since you lost the scimitar and laser pistol like the amateur you are. And we won't be getting any of Aziza's delectable meals in Mexico, so we'll need some rations. And it might not be a bad idea to bring a vomit bag this time."